Dear Bio,

May you ha[ve] ... life ahead. I hope you become wise & courageous like Emma and help others

Nyxa Shah
April 5th 2019

To my children Nikki & Jay

*Without you both, tomorrow wouldn't be worth the wait
and yesterday wouldn't be worth remembering!*

Emma and Friends-Izzy the Bully

Emma

Izzy

Hazel

Oscar

Emma was a bear cub. She lived with her mother, father, and baby brother in a large forest.

Emma was very nice and everyone liked her. Emma was also very wise and other cubs came to her for advice.

One day a new family moved into the forest. They had one bear cub named Izzy.

Izzy was polite and sweet in front of her teachers and other adults.

But Izzy was not so sweet or polite with other cubs. She stole things, made fun of others, pulled pranks, and bossed everyone. Izzy was not a very nice cub.

One afternoon some friends approached Emma. They told her all about Izzy's latest pranks and asked for advice on dealing with Izzy.

Emma listened quietly and pondered over the question. Her eyes lit up as an idea came to her. "Why don't we throw her a party?"

Everyone began talking at once. "But she's not nice!" "She pulled my hair." "She kicked me."

Emma held up a hand. The cubs fell silent. "What if you had to move to a new place? Wouldn't you be unhappy? What if you had to leave all your friends behind? Wouldn't you be sad?" Emma looked at her friends.

"But if she wants to be our friend, why isn't she nice to us?" Oscar, Emma's best friend, asked.

"Maybe because she's afraid of being told no." Emma replied.

Hazel, Emma's other best friend, piped in.
"Then let's have a super party for her."
All the cubs nodded.

It was decided. The party would be held on the following Sunday. The cubs used their allowance to buy seeds, berries, and honey. Lots and lots of honey!

They also made a colorful invitation card for Izzy.

On the night before the party, Emma knocked on Izzy's door.

"What do you want?" Izzy asked. Emma ignored her rudeness and held out the card.

Izzy hesitated, then took the card and opened it. She was very surprised.

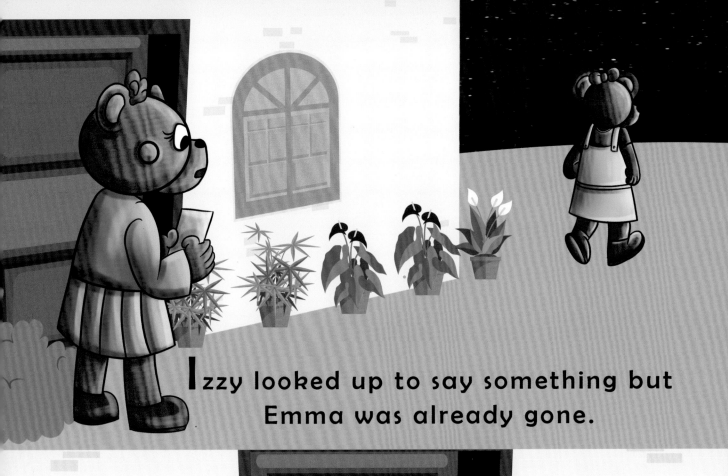

Izzy looked up to say something but Emma was already gone.

Izzy blinked back tears and hugged the card.

The day of the party was warm and sunny.
The party started on time.
Everyone was in good spirits.

The cubs were dancing, playing games, and enjoying the abundance of refreshments.

But where was Izzy?
"Maybe she won't come." Hazel sounded worried.
But Emma was sure Izzy would come.

"I see her coming!" Oscar shouted and started coming down the tall banyan tree he had climbed to be the lookout.

The friends gathered together and waited.

When Izzy saw the large crowd, she stopped, looking nervous.

Emma went to Izzy and took her arm. Drawing Izzy towards the waiting friends, Emma said to her,"Welcome to the neighborhood!"

All the bear cubs also shouted, "Welcome to the neighborhood, Izzy!"